Shortcut
Donald Crews

A Mulberry Paperback Book
New York

Watercolor and gouache
paints were used for
the full-color art.
An airbrush was
used for accents.
The text type is
Futura Bold Italic.

Inquiries should be
addressed to
Greenwillow Books,
a division of
William Morrow &
Company, Inc.,
1350 Avenue of the Americas,
New York, NY 10019.

Printed in the United
States of America.
First Mulberry Edition, 1994.
10 9 8 7 6 5 4 3

The Library of Congress
has cataloged the
Greenwillow edition as
follows:
Crews, Donald.
Shortcut / by Donald Crews.
p. cm.
Summary:
Children taking a shortcut
by walking along a
railroad track find
excitement and danger
when a train approaches.
Mulberry ISBN 0-688-13576-5
[1. Railroads—Fiction.
2. Afro-Americans—Fiction.]
1. Title.
PZ7.C8682Sh 1992
[E]—dc20
91-36312 CIP AC

To Mama/Daddy
Brother/Shirley
Mary
Sylvester/Edward
Sylvia

All's well
that
ends well

We looked....
We listened....
We decided to take
the shortcut home.

We *should* have taken the road.
But it was late, and it was
getting dark, so we
started down the track.

WHOO

We knew when the passenger trains
passed. But the freight trains
didn't run on schedule.
They might come at any time.

We should have taken the road.

WHOO-WHOO

The track ran along a mound. Its steep slopes were covered with briers. There was water at the bottom, surely full of snakes.

We laughed. We shouted. We sang. We tussled. We threw stones. We passed the cut-off that led back to the road.

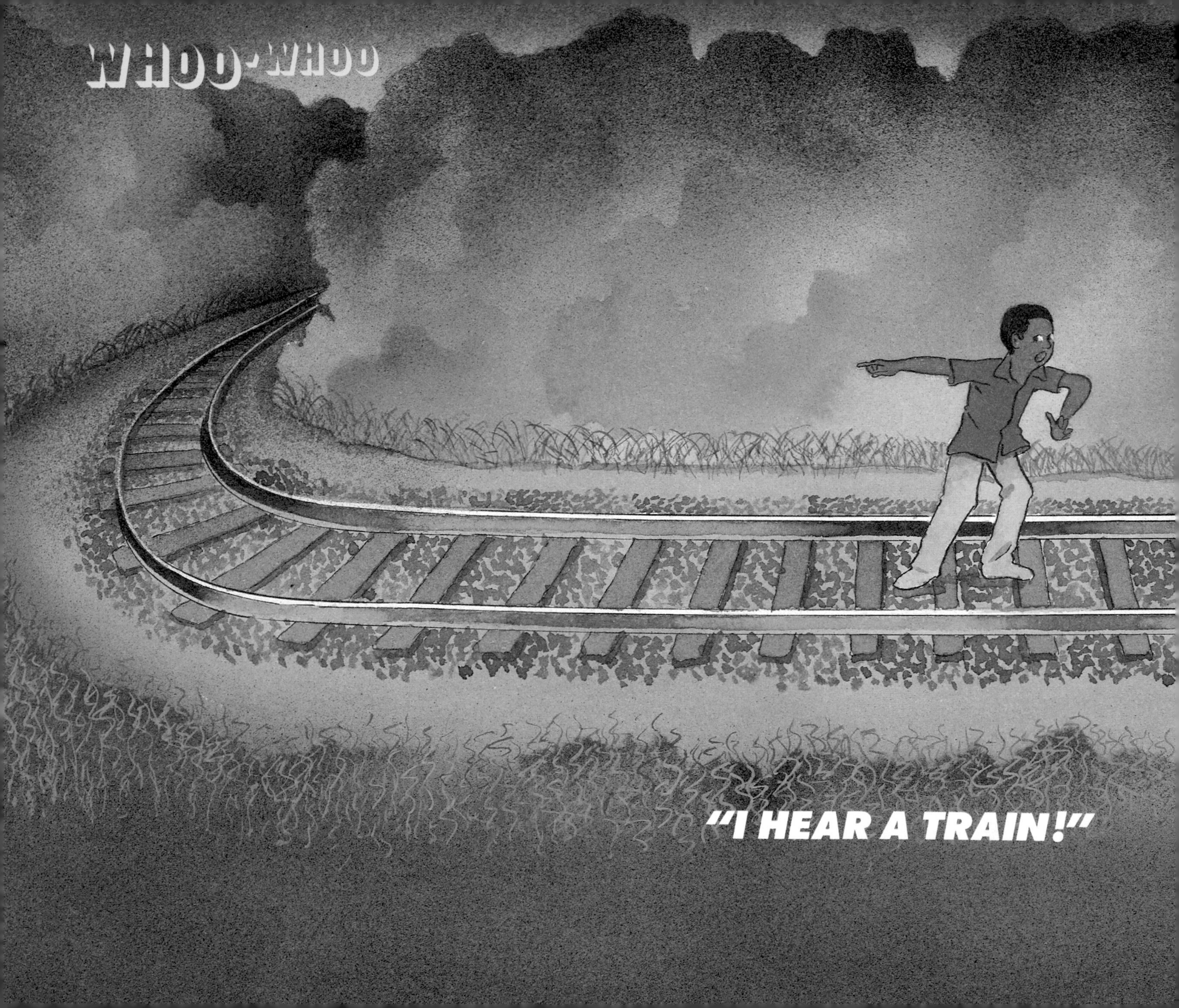
WHOO-WHOO
"I HEAR A TRAIN!"

Everybody stopped.
Everybody listened.
We all heard the train whistle.
Should we run ahead to the
path home or back to the cut-off?

The train whistle was **much louder.**

We jumped off the tracks onto the steep slope. We didn't think about the briers or the snakes.

The train passed.
We were all fine.
We climbed back onto the tracks.
We hurried to the cut-off
and onto the road.

We walked home without a word.
We didn't tell Bigmama. We didn't tell Mama.
We didn't tell anyone. We didn't talk about
what had happened for a very long time.
And we didn't take the short-cut again.